SHADOWS OF MANHATTAN

Dr. Maxwell Shimba

Printed by Shimba Publishing LLC
Printed in the United States of America

TABLE OF CONTENTS

Preface v

Chapter 01 1

The First Body 1

Chapter 02 6

Hidden Secrets 6

Chapter 03 12

The Second Murder 12

Chapter 04 19

A Shaowy Figure 19

Chapter 05 28

The Unraveling 28

Chapter 06 34

The Calm Before the Storm 34

Chapter 07 41

Beneath the Surface 41

Chapter 08 48

Deeper into the Abyss 48

Chapter 09 55

Unraveling the Network 55

Chapter 10 62

The Domino Effect 62

Chapter 11 68

The Web Tightens 68

Chapter 12 74

The Inside Man 74

Chapter 13 82

The Final Countdown..**82**

Chapter 14..**88**

Unfinished Business..**88**

Chapter 15..**95**

A New Dawn..**95**

Epilogue..**102**

PREFACE

In the sprawling urban landscape of New York City, where towering skyscrapers cast long shadows over bustling streets, crime and justice dance an eternal tango. This novel delves into that very dance, exploring the intricate, often perilous journey of two detectives committed to maintaining order amidst chaos.

Detective Alex Carter and Detective Maria Sanchez are not just characters on a page; they embody the relentless spirit of law enforcement officers everywhere. Their story is one of dedication, resilience, and the unyielding pursuit of truth. From the moment they step into the chilling scene of a high-end apartment murder to their strategic takedown of a formidable crime network, Alex and Maria navigate a labyrinth of deceit, danger, and moral dilemmas.

"The First Body" begins with a grisly discovery that sets off a chain of events, unraveling a complex web of corruption and power. As the narrative unfolds, readers are drawn into the meticulous process of detective work—analyzing clues, interviewing suspects, and piecing together fragments of evidence to construct a coherent picture of the truth. The protagonists' personal lives intertwine with their professional duties, highlighting the sacrifices and challenges that come with the badge.

This novel is more than a crime thriller; it is a tribute to the unsung heroes who work tirelessly to protect and serve. It examines the human elements behind the badge, exploring themes of loyalty, trust, and the moral complexities inherent in the pursuit of justice. Alex and Maria's journey is fraught with tension and conflict, yet it is also marked by moments of triumph and camaraderie that underscore the resilience of the human spirit.

In crafting this story, I drew inspiration from the real-world challenges faced by law enforcement officers. The dedication to their mission, often at great personal cost, serves as a powerful reminder of the thin blue line that stands between order and anarchy. This novel seeks to capture that essence, presenting a realistic yet gripping portrayal of detective work in one of the world's most dynamic cities.

I invite you to step into the world of Alex Carter and Maria Sanchez, to walk the beat with them, and to experience the highs and lows of their journey. Through their eyes, may you gain a deeper appreciation for the complexities of justice and the unwavering determination it demands.

Welcome to their story—a tale of courage, perseverance, and the unending quest for truth in the heart of New York City.

Dr. Maxwell Shimba

DR. MAXWELL SHIMBA

CHAPTER 01

THE FIRST BODY

The soft hum of the city was the only sound in the early morning air as Detective Alex Carter sipped his coffee. The taste was bitter, but it was the jolt he needed to start another long day. He glanced around the bustling precinct, where officers and detectives moved with purpose, their faces reflecting the weight of New York City's endless demands.

His partner, Detective Maria Sanchez, walked in, her dark hair pulled into a tight bun and a determined look in her eyes. She handed him a file, her expression grim. "We've got a call. High-end apartment on the Upper East Side. Looks like a bad one."

Alex nodded, tossing his coffee cup into the trash and grabbing his coat. The ride to the crime scene was silent, the gravity of the situation settling over them. They arrived at a luxury apartment building, the flashing lights of police cars casting eerie shadows on the pavement.

Inside, the air was thick with tension. Uniformed officers stood guard, their faces pale. Alex and Maria ducked under the crime scene tape and entered the apartment. The smell of blood hit them first, metallic and overwhelming.

The living room was immaculate, a stark contrast to the horror that awaited them in the study. There, slumped over a mahogany desk, was the body of a man in his fifties. His throat had been slit, and blood pooled on the polished wood. The sight was gruesome, but what caught Alex's attention was the message scrawled on the wall in blood: "Justice for the Damned."

Maria exhaled sharply, her hand covering her mouth. "This is...something else."

Alex approached the body, careful not to disturb any evidence. "The victim?"

"Thomas Blake," Maria replied, consulting the file. "A prominent lawyer, known for representing high-profile clients. Looks like someone had a serious grudge."

Alex examined the message again. "Justice for the Damned. It's cryptic, but it's deliberate. This wasn't just a random killing."

The forensic team arrived, led by Dr. Emily Harris, who immediately began her work on the body. "We'll need to take him back for a full autopsy, but I can tell you right now, this was done with precision. The killer knew what they were doing."

Maria took a deep breath, scanning the room. "We need to find out who hated Blake enough to do this."

As they searched the apartment, they found signs of Blake's affluent lifestyle—expensive artwork, designer furniture, and a state-of-the-art home security system. Yet, the security footage was missing, the tapes expertly removed.

"Whoever did this knew exactly what they were doing," Alex muttered. "This wasn't a spur-of-the-moment crime. It was planned."

Back at the precinct, Alex and Maria began the arduous task of piecing together Blake's life. They interviewed colleagues, clients, and acquaintances. The picture that emerged was of a man who was both revered and reviled. He had made powerful friends and even more powerful enemies.

Their investigation led them to Blake's law firm, a sleek office in a downtown skyscraper. They met with Blake's partner, David Reynolds, a man in his late forties with sharp features and a colder demeanor.

"Thomas was a brilliant lawyer," Reynolds said, though his tone lacked warmth. "But he made a lot of enemies. Comes with the territory."

"Enemies like who?" Maria asked, leaning forward.

Reynolds sighed. "Clients who felt he didn't do enough, rivals who wanted his clients, even some of our own staff who thought he was too hard on them. Take your pick."

As they left the office, Maria frowned. "Reynolds isn't telling us everything. He's hiding something."

"We'll keep digging," Alex replied. "Someone out there knows why Blake was targeted."

Their next stop was Blake's home, where they hoped to find more clues. They searched his personal office, going through files and documents. In a locked drawer, they found a stack of letters, all signed with the initials 'J.D.' The letters were filled with threats and accusations, each one more menacing than the last.

"Justice for the Damned," Alex murmured, holding up one of the letters. "J.D. Whoever this is, they had a serious vendetta against Blake."

The discovery of the letters added a new layer to the mystery. As Alex and Maria delved deeper, they realized they were dealing with a killer who had a personal mission, someone who believed they were serving justice in their own twisted way.

Their investigation was far from over, and with each step, the danger grew. But Alex and Maria were determined to uncover the truth, no matter the cost. Little did they know, the path they were on would lead them into the darkest corners of the city, where shadows concealed deadly secrets and the line between justice and vengeance blurred beyond recognition.

CHAPTER 02

HIDDEN SECRETS

Detective Alex Carter and Detective Maria Sanchez were back at the precinct, surrounded by the noise and chaos that came with solving homicides in New York City. The letters signed 'J.D.' were laid out in front of them, each one a testament to the deep-seated hatred someone harbored against Thomas Blake.

"Who is 'J.D.'?" Maria asked, her brow furrowed in concentration. "We need to figure out their connection to Blake."

Alex nodded. "Let's start by going through Blake's case files. Maybe one of his clients or adversaries used those initials."

They split the workload, each taking a stack of files. Hours passed as they sifted through mountains of legal documents, but nothing seemed to jump out. The initials 'J.D.' were conspicuously absent from Blake's professional life.

Frustrated, Alex leaned back in his chair. "If 'J.D.' isn't connected to his work, then it must be personal. We need to dig into his personal life."

Their first stop was Blake's widow, Evelyn Blake. She lived in a luxurious brownstone in Brooklyn, far removed from the chaos of Manhattan. When they arrived, Evelyn greeted them with red-rimmed eyes and a hollow expression.

"Mrs. Blake, we're very sorry for your loss," Alex began gently. "We need to ask you some questions about your husband's personal life."

Evelyn nodded, her voice barely a whisper. "Thomas was a difficult man. He had many enemies, but I never thought it would come to this."

"Did Thomas ever mention someone with the initials 'J.D.'?" Maria asked.

Evelyn's eyes widened slightly, a flicker of recognition. "J.D... Yes, those were the initials of a man who wrote to

Thomas frequently. The letters were always filled with anger and threats. Thomas never took them seriously, though. He said it was just another disgruntled client."

"Do you have any idea who this person might be?" Alex pressed.

Evelyn shook her head. "No, Thomas was always very private about his work. But I remember him mentioning a case a few years ago that haunted him. It involved a wrongful conviction. He managed to get the conviction overturned, but it ruined someone's life. I think the person's name was James Daniels."

Alex and Maria exchanged glances. "Thank you, Mrs. Blake. You've been very helpful."

Back at the precinct, they began searching for information on James Daniels. It didn't take long to find the case file. James Daniels had been wrongfully convicted of embezzlement, and Blake had successfully overturned the conviction. However, the damage to Daniels' reputation and life had already been done.

"Looks like we have a prime suspect," Maria said. "Daniels had his life destroyed and, even though Blake got him off, he might still blame Blake for not doing enough to prevent the conviction in the first place."

"Let's bring him in for questioning," Alex agreed.

The address listed for James Daniels was a modest apartment in Queens. They drove over and knocked on the door. A gaunt man in his late forties answered, his eyes wary and haunted.

"Mr. Daniels, we're Detectives Carter and Sanchez. We'd like to ask you a few questions about Thomas Blake," Alex said.

Daniels' expression darkened at the mention of Blake. "Why? What's happened?"

"He's been murdered," Maria stated bluntly. "We found letters from someone with the initials 'J.D.' at his apartment. We believe you might have some information."

Daniels' face paled, and he stepped back, allowing them to enter. "I didn't kill him. I hated him, sure, but I didn't murder him."

"Then why the letters?" Alex asked.

Daniels sighed, sinking into a worn-out chair. "After I was exonerated, my life was still in shambles. I lost everything—my job, my family, my reputation. I wrote those letters out of anger, hoping to get some kind of response, some acknowledgment of what I lost. But I didn't kill him. I've moved past that anger."

"Do you have an alibi for the night of the murder?" Maria inquired.

Daniels nodded. "I was at my sister's place in Jersey. We had a family dinner. You can check with her."

They took down the sister's information and left the apartment. On the drive back, Alex mulled over Daniels' words. "What if Daniels is telling the truth? What if someone else is using 'J.D.' to throw us off?"

Maria agreed. "We need to verify his alibi, but we should also consider other possibilities. Blake had a lot of enemies. This could be a smokescreen."

When they reached the precinct, they called Daniels' sister, who confirmed his alibi. It checked out, putting Daniels out of the picture for the time being. The detectives were back to square one, with more questions than answers.

"Let's go back to the beginning," Alex suggested. "We need to re-examine everything—Blake's recent cases, his personal connections. There's something we're missing."

The hours stretched into the night as they pored over documents and interviewed more people connected to Blake. The pieces of the puzzle were scattered and elusive, each new lead bringing them closer to a truth that was darker and more twisted than they could have imagined.

As dawn approached, Maria rubbed her eyes and looked at Alex. "We're dealing with someone meticulous and patient. Someone who planned this down to the last detail."

Alex nodded, his mind racing. "And until we find that person, no one connected to Blake is safe. We need to stay ahead of them, find the pattern before they strike again."

In the silence of the early morning, the detectives knew one thing for certain—their hunt for a killer had only just begun.

CHAPTER 03

THE SECOND MURDER

The next day, Detective Alex Carter and Detective Maria Sanchez were back at the precinct, still grappling with the loose ends of Thomas Blake's murder. They were reviewing potential suspects and following up on leads when their phones rang simultaneously.

"Another body," Alex said, hanging up. "Similar scene. Let's go."

The address led them to a penthouse apartment in Tribeca. As they arrived, the sight was all too familiar: police cars, flashing lights, and a growing crowd of curious onlookers. They flashed their badges and were quickly ushered inside.

In the lavish living room, the scene was eerily similar to the first murder. The victim, a woman in her thirties, lay sprawled on a plush white rug, her throat slit. Her name was Rachel Moore, a wealthy socialite with a list of influential connections. On the wall, written in blood, was the same message: "Justice for the Damned."

Maria shook her head in disbelief. "It's the same signature. We have a serial killer on our hands."

Alex nodded grimly. "We need to dig deeper into the connections between Blake and Moore. This is no coincidence."

The forensic team was already at work, led again by Dr. Emily Harris. "Same method," she confirmed. "Clean, precise. This killer knows what they're doing."

"Any immediate clues?" Alex asked.

"Not much different from Blake's scene," Dr. Harris replied. "We're processing everything now."

Alex and Maria began canvassing the area, speaking to neighbors and staff in the building. One neighbor mentioned seeing a man in a dark hoodie lingering near the elevator earlier that evening, but no one had gotten a good look at him.

Back at the precinct, the detectives began to piece together Rachel Moore's life. She was a prominent figure in New York's social scene, known for her charity work and high-profile relationships. They quickly discovered she had been a client of Thomas Blake, who had represented her in a messy divorce a year ago.

"Blake and Moore were connected," Maria said, pointing to the files spread across the desk. "But that's not enough. We need to find out who had a motive to kill them both."

As they dug deeper, they found that Moore's ex-husband, Robert Caldwell, had a history of violent behavior and had made numerous threats against her. They brought Caldwell in for questioning.

Sitting in the interrogation room, Caldwell was a picture of arrogance. "I didn't kill Rachel," he said flatly. "Why would I? I've moved on. Besides, I was at a business dinner last night. Plenty of witnesses."

"Your ex-wife and Thomas Blake are both dead, murdered in the same brutal fashion," Alex said, leaning in. "And you had a motive for both."

Caldwell smirked. "That's a stretch, detective. You've got nothing on me."

Maria's voice was cold. "We'll be checking your alibi. Don't leave town."

As Caldwell was escorted out, Alex turned to Maria. "What do you think?"

"He's hiding something," Maria said. "But he might not be our killer. We need to verify his alibi."

Their investigation led them to a high-end restaurant in Midtown, where Caldwell's business dinner had taken place. The staff confirmed his presence, and several associates vouched for him, putting him out of the picture for the time being.

Frustration mounted as they returned to the precinct. "We're missing something," Alex said, pacing. "There has to be a link between these victims beyond Blake's professional connection."

"Maybe we're looking at this the wrong way," Maria suggested. "What if the connection isn't about the victims themselves, but about what they represent?"

"Justice for the Damned," Alex murmured, staring at the messages left at the crime scenes. "This killer sees themselves as an avenger. We need to look into Blake's and Moore's pasts—anyone they wronged, any cases that went bad."

They spent the next few days combing through records, talking to former clients, colleagues, and anyone who might have a grudge. They found a few disgruntled clients, but nothing that stood out. Then, an old case file caught Maria's eye.

"Look at this," she said, handing the file to Alex. It was an old case involving a young man named Jacob Delaney, who had been wrongfully convicted of assault. Blake had represented him and eventually got the conviction overturned, but Delaney's life had been destroyed in the process. He had disappeared from the public eye shortly after.

"J.D.," Alex said, realization dawning. "Jacob Delaney. It fits."

They tracked down Delaney's last known address, a rundown apartment in the Bronx. The landlord confirmed that Delaney had lived there but had moved out abruptly a few months ago. A neighbor mentioned seeing Delaney around the building recently, despite supposedly having moved out.

Alex and Maria decided to stake out the building, hoping Delaney would return. After hours of waiting, their patience paid off. A man fitting Delaney's description approached the building, looking around nervously before slipping inside.

They followed him quietly, catching him by surprise as he entered his old apartment. Delaney's face was gaunt, his eyes wild with fear and anger. "What do you want?" he spat, backing away.

"We're detectives Carter and Sanchez," Alex said, showing his badge. "We need to talk to you about Thomas Blake and Rachel Moore."

Delaney's expression twisted with rage. "I didn't kill them. They ruined my life, but I didn't kill them."

"Then why were you hiding?" Maria asked, stepping closer.

Delaney's shoulders slumped. "Because someone is trying to frame me. I got letters, threats, saying if I didn't disappear, I'd be next. They said I had to pay for what happened, just like Blake and Moore."

"Do you still have those letters?" Alex asked.

Delaney nodded, retrieving a stack of crumpled papers from a drawer. The handwriting matched the letters found at the crime scenes. "I don't know who's doing this, but they want me dead."

Alex and Maria exchanged a look. "We need to get you somewhere safe," Alex said. "And we need to find this killer before they strike again."

With Delaney's help, they began to piece together the final clues of a puzzle that was as chilling as it was intricate. The realization that someone else was orchestrating this deadly game from the shadows sent a shiver down their spine. The hunt for justice had only intensified, and the stakes were higher than ever.

CHAPTER 04

A SHAOWY FIGURE

With Jacob Delaney in protective custody, Detective Alex Carter and Detective Maria Sanchez felt the urgency of their task pressing down on them. Someone was out there, meticulously framing Delaney while executing a twisted form of justice on Thomas Blake and Rachel Moore. The question now was who—and why.

Their first lead came from the letters Delaney had received. Forensic analysis revealed traces of a unique ink used by a specific brand of high-end pens, narrowing down potential sources. Alex and Maria canvassed stationery shops and specialty stores across the city, hoping for a breakthrough.

At a small boutique in Midtown, they finally caught a break. The shop owner, an elderly man with a keen eye for detail, recognized the handwriting on the letters. "I've seen this writing before," he said, squinting at the photocopies. "A man came in several months ago, bought a few of these pens. Seemed particular about them."

"Do you remember anything about him?" Maria asked, hopeful.

The owner nodded slowly. "Middle-aged, well-dressed, but something about him was...off. I remember he paid in cash and didn't say much, but he dropped a business card when he left."

"Do you still have it?" Alex inquired.

The owner rummaged through a drawer and produced an old card. "Here it is. I knew it might be important someday."

The card belonged to a private investigator named Samuel Pierce. Alex and Maria exchanged glances, their instincts buzzing. "Thank you, sir. You've been very helpful."

They tracked down Pierce's office, a nondescript building in a quieter part of Manhattan. The receptionist, a sharp-looking woman, greeted them with a wary smile. "Can I help you?"

"We're Detectives Carter and Sanchez," Alex said, showing his badge. "We need to speak with Mr. Pierce."

"He's not in today," she replied smoothly. "Can I take a message?"

"We'll wait," Maria said firmly, sensing the receptionist's reluctance.

They sat in the waiting area, observing the comings and goings of other clients. After what seemed like hours, a tall man in his late forties walked in. He had an air of confidence, but his eyes were cold and calculating. "Detectives, I'm Samuel Pierce. How can I help you?"

"We're investigating the murders of Thomas Blake and Rachel Moore," Alex began. "We have reason to believe you might have information relevant to our case."

Pierce's expression remained neutral. "I'm not sure how I can help. I handle a lot of clients and cases. What makes you think I'm involved?"

"We found letters at the crime scenes written with ink from a specific brand of pens," Maria explained. "Pens you purchased a few months ago."

Pierce raised an eyebrow. "That's quite a stretch, don't you think? A lot of people buy those pens."

"We also have a witness who saw you," Alex added. "And your business card was found at one of the stores."

Pierce's demeanor shifted slightly, a flicker of annoyance crossing his face. "I see. Well, I assure you, I have nothing to do with these murders. I've been conducting my own investigations, unrelated to your case."

"Mind telling us what those investigations involve?" Maria asked, her tone probing.

"Client confidentiality, I'm afraid," Pierce said smoothly. "Unless you have a warrant, I can't disclose anything."

Frustrated but not defeated, Alex and Maria left Pierce's office. "He's hiding something," Maria said as they walked back to their car. "We need to dig deeper into his background."

They began to investigate Pierce's past cases and clients, looking for any connection to Blake or Moore. What they found was a trail of discreet but aggressive investigations, often targeting individuals with dubious pasts or those involved in high-stakes legal battles.

"He's been digging up dirt on people for years," Alex said, scanning through files. "But why would he turn to murder now?"

"Maybe he's been hired by someone," Maria speculated. "Someone who wants revenge and is using Pierce's skills to frame Delaney."

Their next stop was the office of a prominent criminal defense attorney, Lisa Howard, who had frequently employed Pierce's services. She greeted them with professional courtesy but seemed on edge.

"Detectives, what can I do for you?" she asked, motioning for them to sit.

"We're looking into Samuel Pierce and his connection to Thomas Blake and Rachel Moore," Alex said directly. "We believe he might be involved in their murders."

Howard's eyes widened slightly, but she quickly regained her composure. "That's a serious accusation. I hired Pierce for private investigations, nothing more. If he's involved in anything illegal, I'm unaware of it."

"Do you know of anyone who might have hired Pierce to go after Blake or Moore?" Maria asked.

Howard hesitated, glancing around her office. "There was a client, a wealthy businessman named Victor Lang. He had dealings with Blake and Moore that went sour. He hired Pierce to gather information, but that's all I know."

"Can you give us more details about Lang?" Alex asked.

Howard provided Lang's address and contact information, clearly anxious to distance herself from the situation. The detectives thanked her and left, their minds racing with possibilities.

Victor Lang lived in a penthouse overlooking Central Park. The contrast between his opulent lifestyle and the gruesome murders they were investigating was stark. They arrived at his building, showing their badges to the doorman who reluctantly allowed them up.

Lang greeted them in his spacious living room, his demeanor calm and unbothered. "Detectives, to what do I owe the pleasure?"

"We're investigating the murders of Thomas Blake and Rachel Moore," Maria began. "We understand you had business dealings with both."

Lang's smile faded slightly. "Unfortunate business, yes. But I had nothing to do with their deaths."

"Your name came up in connection with Samuel Pierce," Alex added. "We believe he might be involved in the murders."

Lang's expression hardened. "I hired Pierce for investigations, not for murder. If he's gone rogue, that's on him, not me."

"Did Pierce provide you with any useful information on Blake or Moore?" Maria asked, her eyes narrowing.

Lang leaned back, considering his words carefully. "He found some dirt, but nothing that justified what happened to them. I was looking for leverage, not blood."

Their interview with Lang yielded little beyond denials and deflections. As they left, Alex's mind churned with frustration. "We need to keep digging. Pierce is the key. If we can break him, we can uncover who's behind this."

The following days were a whirlwind of surveillance and subtle pressure on Pierce's known associates. They hoped to catch him making a mistake, but he was careful, almost as if he anticipated their moves.

Then, one night, a breakthrough came. A junior detective named Marcus found a connection between Pierce and a small storage unit rented under a fake name. Alex and Maria rushed to the location, obtaining a warrant to search the unit.

Inside, they found a trove of documents, photographs, and surveillance equipment. But most crucially, they found a journal—Pierce's journal—detailing his investigations and the ominous shift from private detective to vigilante assassin.

"He's been tracking people he deems unworthy of justice," Maria said, leafing through the pages. "And Blake and Moore were just the beginning."

Among the notes, they found references to meetings with someone labeled 'V.L.'—Victor Lang. The pieces began to fall into place. Lang had hired Pierce not just for information but to enact a twisted form of justice, eliminating those who had wronged him while framing an innocent man.

Armed with this evidence, Alex and Maria prepared to arrest Pierce and confront Lang. The city's shadows had concealed deadly secrets for too long, and now it was time to bring them into the light. The stakes were higher than ever, but the detectives were ready for the final showdown.

CHAPTER 05

THE UNRAVELING

Detective Alex Carter and Detective Maria Sanchez drove to Samuel Pierce's office with a sense of grim determination. The evidence they had uncovered in the storage unit was damning, and it was time to confront the private investigator.

As they arrived, they noticed Pierce's car parked outside. They entered the building, making their way to his office. The receptionist was absent, the door to Pierce's office slightly ajar. Alex pushed it open cautiously.

Pierce was inside, seated at his desk, his face pale but composed. He looked up as they entered, a resigned look in his eyes. "I was expecting you," he said quietly.

"Samuel Pierce, you are under arrest for the murders of Thomas Blake and Rachel Moore," Alex announced, stepping forward.

Pierce raised his hands in surrender. "I knew it would come to this eventually. You found the journal, didn't you?"

"Yes, we did," Maria said, handcuffing him. "And it's enough to put you away for a long time. But we know you weren't acting alone."

Pierce's eyes flickered with something akin to relief. "It was all Lang's idea. He convinced me that what we were doing was justified, that we were delivering true justice. But I see now how wrong I was."

"You'll have a chance to explain everything," Alex said. "But right now, we need to take you in."

As they escorted Pierce out of the building, he remained silent, a broken man caught in a web of his own making. They drove him to the precinct, where he was processed and placed in an interrogation room.

Alex and Maria took a moment to gather their thoughts. "We need to hit Lang hard," Maria said. "He's the mastermind. If we can get Pierce to testify against him, we can take them both down."

They entered the interrogation room, where Pierce sat staring at his hands. "Samuel," Alex began, "we need you to cooperate. Tell us everything about Lang's involvement."

Pierce sighed deeply. "It started about a year ago. Lang approached me, said he needed someone who could dig up dirt on his enemies. He offered me a lot of money, and I accepted. At first, it was just investigations, but then he started talking about justice, about punishing those who had wronged him."

"Did he explicitly tell you to kill Blake and Moore?" Maria asked.

Pierce nodded. "Yes. He said they needed to be made examples of. He provided me with information, locations, everything I needed. He even suggested framing Delaney, said it would divert suspicion."

"Why did you go along with it?" Alex asked, his voice edged with frustration.

"I believed him," Pierce admitted, his voice cracking. "I thought we were doing the right thing, delivering justice where the system had failed. But it was all a lie. I see that now."

"Will you testify against Lang?" Maria asked.

Pierce hesitated, then nodded. "Yes. I'll do whatever it takes to make this right."

With Pierce's confession in hand, they obtained an arrest warrant for Victor Lang. They coordinated with SWAT, knowing Lang was a dangerous man with resources at his disposal. As they approached his penthouse, the tension was palpable.

SWAT breached the door, flooding the apartment with shouts and the sound of boots on marble floors. Lang was in his study, a glass of whiskey in hand, looking more annoyed than surprised.

"Victor Lang, you're under arrest for conspiracy to commit murder," Alex declared.

Lang smirked, setting his glass down. "Do you really think you can make this stick? I have powerful friends."

"Your friends can't save you from this," Maria said, stepping forward. "We have evidence, we have witnesses, and we have Pierce's testimony. It's over, Lang."

As they cuffed Lang and read him his rights, Alex couldn't shake the feeling that this was far from over. Lang's influence ran deep, and they would need every piece of evidence to ensure he faced justice.

Back at the precinct, they began building their case against Lang. Pierce's testimony was crucial, but they needed to corroborate it with physical evidence and financial records linking Lang to the crimes. They worked tirelessly, knowing Lang's legal team would attack every weak point.

Over the next few weeks, they pieced together a solid case. Financial records showed large transfers from Lang to Pierce, and surveillance footage placed Pierce at the scenes of the murders. They also found emails and messages outlining Lang's twisted plans.

When the case finally went to trial, the courtroom was packed. The media had picked up on the story, and the public was eager to see justice served. Lang's lawyers were relentless, but the evidence was overwhelming. Pierce's heartfelt testimony, combined with the physical evidence, painted a clear picture of Lang's guilt.

In the end, the jury found Lang guilty on all counts. The judge sentenced him to life without parole, ensuring he would never harm anyone again. Pierce received a reduced sentence in exchange for his cooperation, and while he would serve time, there was a sense of closure for the victims' families.

As Alex and Maria left the courthouse, the weight of the case finally lifted. "We did it," Maria said, a small smile breaking through the exhaustion.

"Yeah," Alex agreed, looking up at the city skyline. "But there's always more work to be done."

They returned to the precinct, ready to face whatever came next. In a city as vast and complex as New York, the shadows were never fully banished. But as long as they were on the job, those shadows didn't stand a chance.

CHAPTER 06

THE CALM BEFORE THE STORM

The victory over Victor Lang had brought a sense of relief to the precinct, but Detective Alex Carter and Detective Maria Sanchez knew that their work was far from over. New York City had a way of pulling them back into its darker corners, and the calm after the storm was often short-lived.

Two weeks had passed since Lang's conviction. Alex and Maria returned to their routine cases, but something nagged at Alex. Loose ends from the Lang case lingered in his mind, particularly the way Lang had boasted about his powerful friends. He couldn't shake the feeling that there was more to unravel.

One morning, as they settled in for another day of paperwork, Captain Laura Mitchell called them into her office. She was a no-nonsense leader, her stern expression rarely softened by good news.

"Alex, Maria, good work on the Lang case," Mitchell began, gesturing for them to sit. "But I'm afraid we've got a new situation that needs your attention."

"What's the case, Captain?" Maria asked, her curiosity piqued.

Mitchell handed them a file. "Three bodies found in the East River last night. All had the same distinctive markings carved into their skin. It's not the work of a random killer. We believe it's gang-related."

Alex flipped through the photos. The victims were young, their expressions frozen in terror. The markings were intricate, almost ritualistic. "Any witnesses?"

"None so far," Mitchell replied. "But there's chatter on the street about a new gang making moves. We need you two to get out there, talk to your informants, and find out who's behind this."

Maria nodded. "We're on it."

They left the captain's office, the gravity of their new case settling over them. "Looks like we're diving back into the deep end," Alex said, glancing at the file again.

"Wouldn't have it any other way," Maria replied with a determined smile.

Their first stop was a familiar one: a run-down diner in the Lower East Side. It was a favorite haunt of their informant, Benny "The Rat" Rodriguez. Benny was a small-time crook with a big mouth, always eager to trade information for a bit of leniency.

As they entered the diner, they spotted Benny hunched over a plate of greasy eggs. He looked up, his face lighting up in a forced grin. "Detectives, to what do I owe the pleasure?"

"We need information, Benny," Alex said, sliding into the booth across from him. "Three bodies in the East River, marked up in a pretty specific way. You heard anything?"

Benny's grin faded. He glanced around nervously before leaning in. "Yeah, I've heard whispers. There's a new player in town, calling themselves the Black Vipers. Word is, they're making a move to control the drug trade in the city. Those markings? It's their signature."

"Who's leading them?" Maria asked, her tone serious.

Benny shrugged. "No one knows for sure. They keep their operations tight, but there's a name floating around: Reaper. Real piece of work, from what I hear."

"Reaper?" Alex repeated, jotting down the name. "Any idea where we can find him?"

"Last I heard, they're operating out of an abandoned warehouse in the Bronx. But be careful, Detectives. These guys don't mess around."

"Thanks, Benny," Maria said, sliding a few bills across the table. "Stay out of trouble."

With a potential lead in hand, Alex and Maria headed to the Bronx. The warehouse Benny mentioned was a decaying structure, a relic of the city's industrial past. They parked a few blocks away and approached on foot, the neighborhood eerily quiet.

"This feels like a setup," Alex muttered, scanning the area.

"Stay sharp," Maria replied, her hand resting on her holstered gun.

As they neared the warehouse, they spotted movement inside. Shadows flitted past broken windows, and the faint hum of conversation drifted out. Alex gestured for Maria to follow him around the back, where they found a partially open door.

They slipped inside, the air thick with the scent of decay and something else—fear. They moved quietly through the darkened hallways, following the voices. They came to a large room, dimly lit by a single hanging bulb. A group of men stood around a table, weapons and drugs strewn across its surface.

One of the men, taller and more imposing than the others, was giving orders. His face was obscured by the shadows, but his voice was cold and authoritative. "Reaper," Alex whispered.

Suddenly, a floorboard creaked under Maria's foot. The men turned, their eyes locking onto the intruders. "We've got company!" one of them shouted.

Chaos erupted. Alex and Maria ducked behind a stack of crates as gunfire shattered the silence. They returned fire, methodically working their way towards the group. Alex took down one of the gang members, while Maria disarmed another with a well-placed shot.

Reaper, realizing his position was compromised, made a break for the exit. Alex saw him and gave chase, Maria covering his back. They burst out into the alleyway, the night air filled with the sounds of sirens approaching.

Reaper was fast, but Alex was determined. He tackled the gang leader, bringing him to the ground. They struggled briefly before Alex managed to cuff him. "You're under arrest, Reaper," he said, hauling the man to his feet.

Maria caught up, slightly winded but triumphant. "Nice work, partner."

As they waited for backup to arrive, Reaper glared at them with a mix of anger and defiance. "You think this ends with me?" he spat. "You've got no idea what's coming."

Alex and Maria exchanged a look, the weight of Reaper's words sinking in. They had taken down a key player, but the battle was far from over. The Black Vipers were a new and dangerous force in the city, and their influence was growing.

Back at the precinct, they processed Reaper, his real name revealed as Marcus Tate. He had a long rap sheet, but nothing compared to the atrocities they suspected he had committed. As they debriefed Captain Mitchell, the urgency of their mission became clear.

"This is just the beginning," Mitchell said, her expression grim. "The Black Vipers are planning something big, and we need to stop them before they can do more damage."

Alex nodded. "We'll get to the bottom of this, Captain. We won't let them terrorize our city."

As they prepared for the next phase of their investigation, Alex couldn't help but think about Lang's words. The shadows in New York were deep and dangerous, but as long as he and Maria were on the case, they would keep fighting to bring light to the darkness.

CHAPTER 07

BENEATH THE SURFACE

The precinct buzzed with renewed energy following Marcus "Reaper" Tate's arrest. However, Detectives Alex Carter and Maria Sanchez knew this was only a temporary victory. The Black Vipers were still out there, and their network was likely far more extensive than they had initially imagined.

"Reaper wasn't working alone," Alex said as he and Maria sat down in the briefing room. "We need to cut off the head of the snake before it strikes again."

Maria nodded. "We've got Reaper in custody, but he's not talking. We need to find a way to get to him or locate other members who can lead us to the higher-ups."

Captain Mitchell entered the room, carrying a thick folder. "You're right. Our intelligence team has been working non-stop. We've got a potential lead, but it's risky. There's a club in the Meatpacking District called 'Inferno.' We believe it's a front for the Black Vipers' operations."

Alex raised an eyebrow. "And what's the plan?"

Mitchell laid out a map of the area. "We're sending you in undercover. It's a high-stakes operation, but it's our best shot at gathering intel on the Vipers. We need to identify the key players and find out what they're planning next."

Maria studied the map, nodding slowly. "We'll need solid covers and backup in case things go south."

"Already taken care of," Mitchell assured them. "You'll be posing as a couple of high-rolling investors looking to launder money through their operations. Keep your eyes and ears open, and gather as much information as you can."

That evening, Alex and Maria transformed into their undercover personas. Alex donned a sleek suit, while Maria wore an elegant dress that spoke of wealth and influence. They entered 'Inferno' with an air of confidence, their senses on high alert.

The club was a sensory overload—pulsating lights, throbbing music, and a crowd of people lost in the haze of alcohol and excitement. They navigated through the sea of bodies, making their way to the VIP section. A burly bouncer eyed them suspiciously, but a flash of cash and a confident smile from Alex granted them entry.

Inside the VIP area, the atmosphere was more subdued but no less intense. High-profile patrons mingled, their conversations tinged with hints of illicit dealings. Alex and Maria took seats at a corner table, surveying the room.

"Look for anyone who stands out," Alex murmured, scanning the crowd.

Maria sipped her drink, her eyes sharp. "There, by the bar. The guy with the snake tattoo on his neck. He fits the profile of a Black Viper."

Alex followed her gaze. The man in question was speaking to a group of well-dressed individuals, his body language exuding confidence and authority. "Let's see if we can get closer."

They approached the bar casually, ordering drinks and striking up a conversation with the bartender. After a few minutes, Maria noticed an opportunity. The man with the snake tattoo was alone, his group having dispersed momentarily.

"Mind if we join you?" Maria asked, her tone friendly but assertive.

The man looked up, sizing them up before nodding. "Sure, why not? Name's Viper."

"Nice to meet you, Viper," Alex said, extending a hand. "I'm James, and this is my partner, Alicia. We've heard you're the man to talk to if we're looking to invest in some... lucrative ventures."

Viper's eyes gleamed with interest. "You heard right. We've got a lot going on, and we're always looking for new business partners. What kind of investment are you thinking about?"

"Something big," Maria replied smoothly. "We've got a substantial amount of capital that we need to move discreetly. We're looking for high returns and minimal risk."

Viper leaned in, lowering his voice. "You've come to the right place. But before we get into details, I need to know you're serious. Meet me tomorrow night at this address." He slid a business card across the table.

Alex pocketed the card. "We'll be there."

As they left the club, the weight of their task settled over them. The address on the card was a warehouse in the industrial district—an area known for its secrecy and danger.

The next night, they arrived at the warehouse, dressed in their undercover attire. A few other high-profile cars were parked outside, and they exchanged a look of steely determination before entering.

Inside, the warehouse was a stark contrast to the glitz of the club. It was dimly lit, with an air of foreboding. Viper stood near a table, flanked by several armed men. He gestured for Alex and Maria to approach.

"Glad you could make it," Viper said, his tone businesslike. "We're having a little demonstration tonight. Thought you might want to see what you're getting into."

Alex and Maria exchanged a wary glance but followed Viper to the center of the room. There, bound and gagged, was a terrified man. Viper snapped his fingers, and one of his men stepped forward, brandishing a knife.

"This is what happens to those who betray us," Viper explained coldly. "Consider it a lesson in loyalty."

As the man screamed behind his gag, Alex and Maria fought to maintain their composure. They watched in horror as the enforcer carved the same intricate markings into the man's skin—a grim signature of the Black Vipers.

After the gruesome display, Viper turned to them. "Still interested?"

Alex swallowed hard, his mind racing. "We're in."

"Good," Viper said, a satisfied smirk on his face. "Welcome to the Black Vipers. We'll be in touch with your first assignment."

As they left the warehouse, Alex and Maria knew they had just taken a dangerous step deeper into the heart of the beast. The stakes were higher than ever, but they were determined to see this through and bring the Black Vipers to justice.

Back at the precinct, they debriefed Captain Mitchell, detailing the events of the night. Mitchell's face was grim as she listened. "We need to tread carefully. One wrong move, and they'll know you're cops. But this might be our best chance to take them down from the inside."

Alex nodded. "We're ready, Captain. Whatever it takes."

As they prepared for their next undercover assignment, Alex and Maria knew the road ahead would be fraught with danger. But they were driven by a relentless pursuit of justice, ready to face whatever the shadows of New York City threw their way.

CHAPTER 08

DEEPER INTO THE ABYSS

The following days were a blur of tense preparation and careful infiltration. Detective Alex Carter and Detective Maria Sanchez had officially been inducted into the Black Vipers' inner circle, and the pressure to maintain their covers was immense.

Viper, now known as Andre Vega, had assigned them their first task: oversee a significant drug shipment arriving at the docks. The operation was critical for the Vipers' dominance in the city's drug trade, and any misstep could blow their cover and endanger their lives.

The night of the shipment was cold and foggy, the kind of night where shadows seemed to stretch longer and the air was thick with tension. Alex and Maria arrived at the docks early, their nerves steeled for the task ahead. They were met by Viper's right-hand man, a burly figure named Rico.

"You two handle yourselves well," Rico grunted, handing them a clipboard with the shipment details. "Don't screw this up."

"We won't," Maria replied, her voice steady.

As the cargo ship docked, a group of workers began unloading the crates. Alex and Maria supervised, making sure everything went according to plan. They knew they had to gather as much evidence as possible without arousing suspicion.

"Keep an eye out," Alex whispered to Maria as he pretended to check off items on the clipboard. "We need to get a sense of the scale of this operation."

Maria nodded, her eyes scanning the area. "I see the same symbols from the warehouse on the crates. This is definitely linked to their larger network."

They carefully documented everything with hidden cameras and recording devices. Just as they were about to wrap up, Alex noticed something peculiar—a crate marked with a different symbol. He signaled Maria, and they discreetly moved closer to investigate.

"Looks like a separate shipment," Maria muttered. "We need to see what's inside."

Using the pretext of a routine check, they opened the crate. Inside, they found weapons—high-grade military equipment that no street gang should have access to. Alex's mind raced. This was far beyond the scope of a typical drug operation.

"Who the hell are these guys working with?" Alex whispered, his heart pounding. "This isn't just about drugs. They're gearing up for something big."

Before they could delve further, Rico approached. "Everything in order?"

Alex quickly closed the crate and turned, nodding. "All set. Just a few more checks."

"Good," Rico grunted. "Wrap it up. We've got another meeting tonight."

Later that night, they gathered at an abandoned warehouse, a known meeting spot for the Black Vipers. As

Alex and Maria entered, they were greeted by the sight of Vega and his core team, discussing plans and strategies.

"James, Alicia, glad you could join us," Vega said with a menacing smile. "We've got big plans, and you two are going to play a key role."

Maria forced a smile. "We're ready."

Vega motioned for them to sit. "We've got a major deal coming up. We're expanding our territory, and we need reliable people to oversee our new operations."

As the meeting progressed, Alex and Maria learned about the Vipers' plans to take over rival gang territories and expand their influence in the city. The weapons shipment they had seen was just the beginning.

"We need to find out who's supplying them with these weapons," Alex whispered to Maria when they had a moment alone. "This goes way deeper than we thought."

Maria nodded. "We need to get this information to Mitchell, fast. But we can't risk blowing our cover."

Back at the precinct, they met with Captain Mitchell in a secure room, sharing their findings. Mitchell's expression grew darker with each revelation.

"This is worse than we anticipated," she said. "The Black Vipers aren't just a gang—they're part of a much larger network. We need to figure out who's pulling the strings."

"We need to intercept their next shipment and track it back to the source," Alex suggested. "But we'll need more manpower and resources."

Mitchell agreed. "I'll put together a task force. We can't afford to let this escalate."

The following week was a whirlwind of covert planning and surveillance. Alex and Maria juggled their duties as detectives and undercover operatives, constantly on edge. Every encounter with the Vipers was a balancing act between gaining their trust and gathering intelligence.

The night of the next shipment arrived. This time, the location was a secluded airstrip outside the city. Alex and Maria were tasked with overseeing the transfer of goods from a private plane to waiting trucks.

As they arrived, they saw Vega talking to a man in a suit—someone who didn't fit the usual profile of a gang member. Alex's instincts screamed at him. This was the supplier, or at least someone high up in the chain.

"Keep an eye on that guy," Alex whispered to Maria. "He's the key."

They oversaw the unloading, documenting everything discreetly. Maria managed to snap a few photos of the suited man without being noticed. As the operation wrapped up, Vega approached them.

"You two have done well," he said, a rare compliment from the usually stern leader. "There's a lot more to come, and I expect you to be ready."

"We're always ready," Maria replied, her smile hiding her anxiety.

As they drove back to the city, Alex and Maria reviewed the evidence they had gathered. The photos, the recordings, the shipment logs—it was all coming together.

At the precinct, they presented their findings to Captain Mitchell and the task force. "This is the man we need to focus on," Alex said, pointing to a photo of the suited man. "He's the link between the Vipers and their suppliers."

Mitchell nodded. "We'll run his image through our databases. In the meantime, we need to keep up the pressure.

The Vipers are planning something big, and we need to be one step ahead."

The pressure mounted as Alex and Maria continued their dual roles. Every interaction with the Vipers brought new dangers, but also new opportunities. They were getting closer to the heart of the operation, but the stakes were higher than ever.

As they prepared for their next move, the weight of their mission pressed down on them. The calm before the storm was over, and they were plunging deeper into the abyss. But they were ready to face whatever came their way, driven by their relentless pursuit of justice and their commitment to protecting the city they loved.

CHAPTER 09

UNRAVELING THE NETWORK

The task force had identified the man in the suit from the airstrip photos. His name was Nikolai Petrov, a known arms dealer with connections to various criminal organizations worldwide. This revelation brought a new layer of complexity to the case, suggesting that the Black Vipers were part of an international crime syndicate.

Alex Carter and Maria Sanchez knew they had to move quickly. Their mission now was to gain more intelligence on Nikolai Petrov and his operations. They needed to find out how deeply he was intertwined with the Black Vipers and what his ultimate goals were.

"We need to get closer to Petrov," Alex said during a strategy meeting with Captain Mitchell and the task force. "If we can expose his network, we can cripple the Vipers' supply chain."

Mitchell nodded. "We've got to tread carefully. Petrov is dangerous and well-connected. Any misstep could have serious repercussions."

A week later, Alex and Maria found themselves at another opulent gathering, this time at a mansion in the Hamptons. The event was a masquerade ball, a perfect cover for underworld figures to mingle without revealing their identities. Vega had insisted they attend, hinting that Petrov would be present.

Dressed in elegant evening wear and hidden behind ornate masks, Alex and Maria entered the mansion, their senses heightened. The grand ballroom was filled with masked guests, each one a potential ally or enemy.

"Stay close," Alex whispered to Maria, his eyes scanning the room. "We need to identify Petrov and anyone he's speaking with."

They moved through the crowd, engaging in small talk and blending in. Eventually, they spotted Petrov—recognizable even behind his mask—speaking with a group of men in a secluded corner.

"There he is," Maria murmured. "We need to get closer."

They inched their way toward Petrov, listening intently to his conversation. He spoke in hushed tones, but they caught fragments about a major shipment arriving soon and plans to expand operations into new territories.

"This shipment could be our chance," Alex whispered. "If we can intercept it, we can gather enough evidence to bring him down."

As they continued to eavesdrop, Petrov suddenly turned his gaze toward them. "You there," he called out, his voice thick with a Russian accent. "I don't believe we've met."

Alex's heart skipped a beat, but he maintained his composure. "No, I don't think we have. I'm James, and this is Alicia. Vega told us this would be an interesting event."

Petrov's eyes narrowed behind his mask. "Ah, Vega's new recruits. He speaks highly of you."

"Thank you," Maria replied smoothly. "We're honored to be part of the team."

Petrov studied them for a moment before nodding. "Enjoy the evening. We'll be seeing more of each other, I'm sure."

As Petrov turned back to his group, Alex and Maria exchanged a relieved glance. They had managed to avoid suspicion, but the encounter had underscored the danger they were in.

The next day, they met with Captain Mitchell to debrief and plan their next move. "Petrov mentioned a major shipment arriving soon," Alex reported. "We need to find out where and when."

Mitchell nodded, her expression grave. "We'll increase our surveillance and try to intercept any communications about the shipment. In the meantime, you two need to maintain your covers and gather as much information as possible."

Over the next few days, Alex and Maria juggled their duties as undercover operatives and detectives. The tension was palpable, and every interaction with the Vipers was fraught with danger. They knew that one wrong move could blow their cover and jeopardize the entire operation.

Finally, a breakthrough came. Their surveillance team intercepted a message detailing the arrival of the shipment at a private airfield outside the city. The task force quickly mobilized, preparing for a high-stakes interception.

The night of the operation, Alex and Maria joined the task force at the airfield, their nerves steeled for what lay ahead. The air was thick with anticipation as they took their positions, ready to move in at a moment's notice.

"Remember, we need to catch them red-handed," Mitchell reminded them over the radio. "Our priority is Petrov. We take him down, and the rest will follow."

As the cargo plane landed and the shipment was unloaded, the task force moved in, surrounding the area. Alex and Maria, still in their undercover roles, approached Petrov, who was overseeing the transfer.

"What's going on?" Petrov demanded, his eyes darting around.

"It's a setup," Alex said, his voice calm but urgent. "We need to get out of here."

Petrov hesitated for a moment before nodding. "You're right. Let's move."

As they led Petrov toward a waiting vehicle, the task force closed in, guns drawn. "NYPD! Freeze!"

Petrov's eyes widened in shock as Alex and Maria revealed their badges. "You..."

"Game over, Petrov," Alex said, his voice cold.

Petrov lunged for a gun, but the task force was faster. He was quickly subdued and handcuffed, his face a mask of fury.

Back at the precinct, the atmosphere was electric. The operation had been a success, and Petrov's arrest had dealt a significant blow to the Black Vipers' operations. As they debriefed with Captain Mitchell, Alex and Maria felt a sense of accomplishment but knew their work wasn't over.

"This is a major victory," Mitchell said. "But we need to follow through. Petrov's network is extensive, and we need to dismantle it piece by piece."

Alex nodded. "We're ready, Captain. Whatever it takes."

As they prepared for the next phase of their mission, Alex and Maria knew they were plunging deeper into the abyss. But their resolve was unwavering, driven by their commitment to justice and the desire to protect their city from the shadows that threatened it.

CHAPTER 10

THE DOMINO EFFECT

With Nikolai Petrov behind bars, the task force shifted its focus to dismantling the remaining pieces of his criminal network. Detective Alex Carter and Detective Maria Sanchez were at the forefront of this effort, determined to see their mission through to the end.

Days after Petrov's arrest, the task force worked tirelessly to follow up on every lead. Documents and electronic devices seized during the operation provided a treasure trove of information. The scope of Petrov's network was staggering, with connections to several other criminal organizations and corrupt officials.

Captain Mitchell called a meeting to discuss their next steps. "We have a lot of work ahead of us," she said, addressing the room filled with detectives and agents. "Our priority is to use the information we've gathered to arrest key figures in Petrov's network and cut off their operations."

Alex and Maria were assigned to track down one of Petrov's top lieutenants, a man named Carlos Mendez. Mendez was known for his ruthlessness and had been instrumental in securing the weapons shipments. According to their intelligence, he was hiding out in a safehouse in Brooklyn.

"We need to move quickly," Alex said as they geared up for the raid. "Mendez won't stay in one place for long, especially now that Petrov is in custody."

Maria nodded, checking her weapon. "Let's bring him in."

The operation to capture Mendez was swift and efficient. The task force stormed the safehouse, catching Mendez and his men off guard. After a brief but intense firefight, Mendez was apprehended and taken into custody. His arrest was another significant blow to Petrov's network.

During the interrogation, Mendez was initially uncooperative. But faced with the mounting evidence against him, he eventually started to talk. He revealed details about other key members of the network and their operations.

"This is exactly what we needed," Maria said, reviewing the interrogation transcripts. "Mendez's information will help us take down the rest of the network."

With Mendez's intelligence, the task force launched a series of coordinated raids across the city. Warehouses storing illegal arms, drug distribution centers, and safehouses were all targeted. Each successful operation brought them closer to dismantling Petrov's empire.

As the task force celebrated their victories, Alex couldn't shake the feeling that they were missing something. "Petrov was well-connected and smart," he mused. "There has to be someone else pulling the strings, someone even higher up."

Maria agreed. "We need to dig deeper into Petrov's connections. There could be another player we haven't identified yet."

Their suspicions were confirmed when they uncovered a series of encrypted emails on one of Petrov's seized devices. The emails referenced a mysterious figure known only as "The Broker." The Broker appeared to be a facilitator, coordinating between various criminal enterprises and providing them with resources.

"We need to find out who The Broker is," Alex said, studying the emails. "If we can take them down, we can cripple the entire network."

The task force's tech team worked around the clock to decrypt the emails and trace their origin. After days of relentless effort, they finally got a break. The emails were traced back to an office building in Manhattan.

"This could be it," Maria said, her excitement palpable. "We need to move quickly."

The operation to capture The Broker was meticulously planned. The task force prepared for any eventuality, knowing that this figure would be heavily protected.

As they approached the office building, Alex and Maria felt a familiar mix of anticipation and tension. They entered the building, moving swiftly and silently. They reached the designated floor and found a high-tech office filled with computer equipment and security personnel.

"On my signal," Alex whispered, signaling the team to move in.

The task force stormed the office, overwhelming the guards and securing the area. In the back office, they found

The Broker—a middle-aged woman with an air of calm authority. She offered no resistance as she was handcuffed and led away.

"You have no idea what you're disrupting," she said coolly as Alex read her rights.

"We know enough," Alex replied. "And we'll find out the rest soon enough."

Back at the precinct, The Broker's interrogation began. Her real name was Evelyn Chambers, a former intelligence officer who had used her skills to build a criminal empire. She was confident, almost taunting, as she faced Alex and Maria.

"You think you've won?" she said, a faint smile on her lips. "This network is far-reaching. You can't possibly dismantle it all."

"We've already taken down Petrov and Mendez," Maria replied. "And we'll keep going until every last piece of your network is destroyed."

Evelyn's smile faded slightly, but her confidence remained. "Good luck," she said. "You'll need it."

The task force's work was far from over. The capture of Evelyn Chambers provided them with invaluable intelligence, but it also revealed the vastness of the criminal network they were up against. Alex and Maria knew that the road ahead would be long and difficult, but they were determined to see it through.

As they prepared for the next phase of their mission, they reflected on how far they had come. They had uncovered a web of corruption and crime that reached deeper than they had ever imagined, and they had struck significant blows against it. But the fight was far from over.

"We'll keep pushing," Alex said, his resolve unwavering. "We'll take them all down, one by one."

Maria nodded, her determination matching his. "For the city, and for justice."

And so, they continued their relentless pursuit, knowing that the battle for New York City's soul was just beginning.

CHAPTER 11

THE WEB TIGHTENS

The arrest of Evelyn Chambers, aka The Broker, was a significant victory, but it only marked the beginning of a new, more dangerous phase in the operation. The intelligence gathered from her and the information decrypted from her devices revealed the vast, intricate network she had orchestrated. The task force now faced the daunting challenge of dismantling this sprawling criminal empire.

Alex Carter and Maria Sanchez delved into the new data with renewed vigor. They uncovered connections to high-ranking officials, international smuggling rings, and corrupt business entities. Each lead seemed to branch out into several more, like a hydra with countless heads.

"We need to prioritize," Alex said during a strategy session with Captain Mitchell and the rest of the task force.

"If we spread ourselves too thin, we'll never be able to cut off the main arteries of this network."

Mitchell nodded, her brow furrowed in concentration. "Agreed. Let's focus on the most critical nodes first—those that handle the flow of money and weapons."

Their first target was a seemingly legitimate financial firm downtown, which was a front for laundering money from various illicit activities. According to the decrypted files, this firm was crucial in keeping the network's operations funded.

The task force executed a raid on the firm, seizing documents and computer systems. Alex and Maria personally interrogated the firm's executives, who initially feigned ignorance but quickly crumbled under pressure.

"It's all run through offshore accounts," one of the executives confessed. "The money is funneled through shell companies. You'll need a forensic accountant to trace it all."

The task force brought in financial experts who meticulously traced the flow of funds. Their work led to the exposure of several shell companies and offshore accounts, each linked to different parts of the criminal network. As they began freezing assets and cutting off financial channels, the network's operations started to falter.

"We're making progress," Maria said, reviewing the latest reports. "But we still need to hit their supply lines."

Next, they turned their attention to the weapons smuggling operations. The intelligence pointed to a major shipment scheduled to arrive at a private marina. This shipment was critical for the network's ability to arm its operatives and maintain control over their territories.

The night of the raid on the marina was tense. The task force moved in under the cover of darkness, their approach silent and coordinated. As they breached the perimeter, they encountered heavy resistance. Gunfire erupted, and the night was lit up with muzzle flashes and the sounds of combat.

Alex and Maria led the charge, their focus sharp and their movements precise. They pushed through the resistance, securing the shipment and capturing several key figures involved in the smuggling operation.

"Check those crates," Alex ordered, breathing heavily as the firefight subsided.

Maria pried open one of the crates, revealing an arsenal of military-grade weapons. "This would have armed an army," she said, shaking her head. "We just took a big chunk out of their capabilities."

Back at the precinct, the mood was cautiously optimistic. The task force had dealt significant blows to the network's financial and logistical operations, but they knew the fight was far from over.

"Evelyn Chambers mentioned that the network is vast and resilient," Mitchell reminded them during a debriefing. "We need to keep the pressure on and stay vigilant."

As they sifted through the new intelligence, Alex noticed a recurring name: Viktor Dragovich. Dragovich was a notorious crime lord with ties to various global syndicates, and he seemed to be a key player in Chambers' network.

"This guy is big," Alex said, pointing to Dragovich's file. "If we can take him down, it could cause a major collapse in the network."

Maria nodded. "But he'll be heavily protected. We need a solid plan."

The task force began gathering intel on Dragovich, tracking his movements and identifying his associates. They learned that he operated out of a heavily fortified compound on the outskirts of the city. Taking him down would require meticulous planning and precise execution.

"We need to isolate him from his guards," Alex suggested during a planning session. "If we can create a diversion, we might be able to get close enough to apprehend him."

The plan involved a multi-pronged assault: a diversionary attack to draw away the guards, while a smaller, elite team would infiltrate the compound and capture Dragovich. It was risky, but they had no choice.

The night of the assault, the task force moved with military precision. The diversionary team launched their attack, drawing the guards away from the main compound. Amidst the chaos, Alex, Maria, and a select group of operatives made their move.

They breached the compound's defenses, moving swiftly through the halls. The sound of gunfire and explosions echoed in the distance, but they maintained their focus. Finally, they reached Dragovich's office.

Alex kicked the door open, his gun trained on the crime lord. "Viktor Dragovich, you're under arrest!"

Dragovich sneered, his hands raised. "You think this ends with me? You're just cutting off one head. Another will rise to take my place."

"Maybe," Maria said, handcuffing him. "But we'll keep cutting them off until there's nothing left."

Back at the precinct, the mood was one of cautious triumph. Dragovich's capture was a major victory, but his words lingered in Alex's mind. The network was vast and resilient, but so was the task force's determination.

As they continued their relentless pursuit of justice, Alex and Maria knew that the battle was far from over. But each victory brought them closer to dismantling the criminal empire that threatened their city.

"We're making a difference," Alex said, looking at the wall of evidence and photos. "One piece at a time."

Maria nodded, her eyes filled with resolve. "We'll see this through, no matter how long it takes."

And so, they pressed on, knowing that the web of crime was tightening, but their resolve was stronger than ever.

CHAPTER 12

THE INSIDE MAN

With Viktor Dragovich in custody, the task force's relentless pursuit of justice intensified. The intelligence gathered from Dragovich revealed even more about the vast network orchestrated by Evelyn Chambers, aka The Broker. Each piece of information brought them closer to dismantling the entire criminal empire, but the deeper they dug, the more complex the web became.

Back at the precinct, Alex Carter and Maria Sanchez pored over the latest intelligence. Dragovich's capture had provided them with valuable insights, but it also raised new questions. They needed to find the remaining leaders and disrupt the network's operations before they could regroup and retaliate.

"We're making progress, but we need an insider," Alex said, leaning back in his chair. "Someone who knows the inner workings of the network."

Maria nodded thoughtfully. "Agreed. We've been hitting their operations hard, but we need someone who can give us direct access to their plans and key players."

Their opportunity came sooner than expected. One of the operatives captured during the marina raid, a low-level enforcer named Lucas Martinez, seemed eager to cut a deal. He had been loyal to Dragovich out of fear rather than allegiance and saw an opportunity to save himself.

Captain Mitchell arranged for Alex and Maria to interrogate Martinez. They needed to ensure his information was credible and determine if he could be trusted as an informant.

"Martinez, you have one chance," Alex said, his voice firm. "Give us something we can use, and we'll consider a deal. Otherwise, you're looking at a long time behind bars."

Martinez shifted nervously in his seat. "I want protection. If I talk, they'll come after me."

"You help us, and we'll do our best to protect you," Maria assured him. "But we need solid information—names, locations, plans. Everything."

Martinez hesitated, then nodded. "Alright. There's a meeting happening soon, at a warehouse in the industrial district. The remaining leaders are planning their next move, trying to regroup after all the hits you've made."

The task force prepared for the operation, treating Martinez's information with cautious optimism. If the meeting was as significant as he claimed, it could be their chance to strike a decisive blow against the network.

The warehouse was heavily guarded, with armed men patrolling the perimeter. The task force split into teams, each assigned to different entry points to ensure no one could escape.

Alex and Maria led the main assault team, their nerves steeled for the confrontation ahead. "Remember, our priority is to capture the leaders alive," Alex reminded his team. "We need them to bring down the rest of the network."

They moved in swiftly, breaching the warehouse doors and engaging the guards. The element of surprise worked in their favor, and within minutes, they had secured the area and rounded up the key figures attending the meeting.

Among those captured was Damian Rossi, a notorious figure known for his ruthless tactics and strategic mind. He was one of The Broker's top lieutenants, and his capture was a significant victory.

Back at the precinct, the interrogation of Rossi began. Unlike Martinez, Rossi was defiant and uncooperative. He taunted Alex and Maria, confident that his network was too vast to be dismantled.

"You think you've won?" Rossi sneered. "There are others, more powerful than you can imagine. Taking me down won't change anything."

"You're wrong," Alex replied calmly. "Every piece we take down weakens your network. And we'll keep going until there's nothing left."

Maria leaned forward, her eyes cold. "Tell us about The Broker's contingency plans. We know she anticipated this. What are you planning next?"

Rossi's defiance wavered slightly, but he remained silent. It was clear he wasn't going to break easily.

Despite Rossi's resistance, the task force continued to make headway. Documents and digital files seized from the warehouse provided valuable intelligence on the network's operations and revealed the locations of several hidden safehouses and arms caches.

"We're getting closer," Maria said, reviewing the latest findings. "But we need to stay ahead of them. They're bound to retaliate."

Their next target was a high-security safehouse in Queens, rumored to be a hub for the network's leadership. The task force planned a coordinated raid, aiming to capture as many key figures as possible.

The raid was meticulously planned and executed. The task force moved in with precision, neutralizing the guards and securing the safehouse. Inside, they found more high-ranking members of the network, along with a cache of weapons and documents.

One of the captured leaders was Adrian Blackwood, a financial mastermind who had been instrumental in laundering money for the network. His arrest was another significant blow, and his interrogation promised to yield even more valuable information.

As they celebrated their victories, Alex and Maria knew they couldn't let their guard down. The network was vast and resilient, and every step forward was met with new challenges.

Late one night, as Alex reviewed the day's progress at his desk, he received a call from an unknown number. He answered cautiously. "Carter."

The voice on the other end was distorted, but unmistakably familiar. "Detective Carter, this is Evelyn Chambers. The game isn't over."

Alex's heart raced. "Chambers. You're making a mistake by calling me."

"Am I?" she replied coolly. "You may have captured a few of my associates, but the network is still strong. And I'm still in control."

"We'll see about that," Alex said, trying to keep his voice steady.

"You can't stop us," she continued. "And I'll be watching your every move. Good luck, Detective. You'll need it."

The line went dead, leaving Alex with a renewed sense of urgency and determination. The battle was far from over, but he knew one thing for certain: they had Evelyn Chambers worried. And that meant they were on the right track.

The next morning, Alex briefed the task force on the call. "Chambers is feeling the pressure. We need to keep pushing, hit them harder and faster."

Captain Mitchell nodded. "We've made significant progress, but we can't afford to let up. Let's focus on disrupting their remaining operations and capturing the last of their leadership."

As the task force prepared for the next phase of their mission, Alex and Maria felt a renewed sense of purpose. They were closer than ever to dismantling the criminal empire that had plagued their city, but the final confrontation with Evelyn Chambers loomed large.

"We'll get her," Maria said, her resolve unwavering. "One step at a time."

Alex nodded, his determination matching hers. "And we won't stop until we do."

With the network's leaders falling one by one, the task force knew that the endgame was near. But as they prepared for the final push, they also knew that the most dangerous part of their mission was still ahead.

CHAPTER 13

THE FINAL COUNTDOWN

The capture of several key figures in the criminal network had significantly weakened Evelyn Chambers' operations, but the battle was far from over. With each victory, the stakes grew higher, and the threat of retaliation loomed larger. Detective Alex Carter and Detective Maria Sanchez knew they had to act quickly to dismantle the network completely and bring Evelyn Chambers to justice.

The task force worked around the clock, analyzing the information obtained from the recent arrests. They discovered that Evelyn had set up a series of safehouses and secret meeting points across the city, creating a labyrinth of hideouts that made her difficult to pin down.

"We need to cut off her escape routes and isolate her," Alex said during a strategy meeting with Captain Mitchell and the team. "If we can box her in, we'll have a better chance of capturing her."

Maria nodded. "Agreed. We should focus on her most likely hideouts and set up surveillance. We can't afford to let her slip through our fingers."

The first target was a luxury penthouse in midtown Manhattan, a property linked to a shell company controlled by Evelyn. The task force staked out the location, monitoring the comings and goings of anyone who might be connected to her.

After several days of surveillance, they observed a familiar face entering the building: one of Evelyn's trusted lieutenants, known for handling her security. The task force decided it was time to move in.

The raid on the penthouse was swift and decisive. The team breached the doors, securing the area and apprehending everyone inside. To their surprise, they found not only the lieutenant but also several high-ranking members of the network, including a corrupt politician who had been providing cover for Evelyn's operations.

"Looks like we've hit the jackpot," Maria said, securing the politician's hands behind his back. "This should put even more pressure on Evelyn."

Despite the significant arrests, Evelyn herself was nowhere to be found. However, the documents and electronic devices seized during the raid provided valuable intel on her next moves.

Back at the precinct, Alex and Maria reviewed the new information. Among the files, they found a series of encrypted messages detailing a planned meeting at an abandoned factory on the outskirts of the city. The meeting was scheduled for the following night, and it appeared to be a last-ditch effort for Evelyn to regroup with her remaining allies.

"This could be our chance," Alex said, leaning over the documents. "If we can intercept her there, we might finally be able to bring her in."

Captain Mitchell agreed. "We'll need to be careful. If she's desperate, she could be even more dangerous."

The task force prepared for the operation with meticulous care. They gathered all available resources, coordinating with SWAT teams and other law enforcement agencies to ensure they could cover all possible escape routes.

The plan was to surround the factory, leaving no room for Evelyn to escape.

As night fell, the teams moved into position. The factory was a sprawling, dilapidated structure, its windows broken and walls covered in graffiti. The atmosphere was tense as they waited for the signal to move in.

Inside the factory, Evelyn Chambers paced anxiously, her mind racing with contingency plans. She knew the authorities were closing in, but she was determined to outmaneuver them. Her remaining loyalists were gathered, armed and ready for a fight.

Suddenly, the doors were breached, and the task force stormed in. Chaos erupted as Evelyn's men opened fire, and the air was filled with the sounds of gunfire and shouting.

Alex and Maria led the charge, moving through the factory with precision. They cleared rooms methodically, neutralizing threats and pushing closer to Evelyn's location.

"There she is!" Maria shouted, spotting Evelyn at the far end of the main hall, flanked by her bodyguards.

"Chambers, it's over!" Alex yelled, aiming his weapon at her.

Evelyn smirked, her eyes cold and calculating. "You think you've won, Detective? This isn't the end."

Before she could say more, one of her bodyguards lunged at Alex, forcing him to engage in a brutal hand-to-hand fight. Maria covered him, taking down another guard as she advanced toward Evelyn.

The fight was intense, but Alex managed to overpower his opponent, knocking him unconscious. He turned just in time to see Maria closing in on Evelyn, who was attempting to flee through a side exit.

"Stop right there, Chambers!" Maria shouted, her voice echoing through the hall.

Evelyn paused, realizing she was cornered. With a resigned sigh, she raised her hands, dropping the gun she had been holding.

"You've made quite a mess, Detective," she said, her tone dripping with disdain.

"And now it's over," Maria replied, handcuffing her. "You're under arrest."

With Evelyn Chambers in custody, the task force breathed a collective sigh of relief. The operation had been a success, but they knew the work wasn't done yet. They still needed to ensure that every aspect of her network was dismantled and that justice was served.

Back at the precinct, Alex and Maria processed the gravity of their achievement. They had taken down one of the most formidable criminal empires the city had ever seen, but they also knew that vigilance was key to preventing such a network from rising again.

"We did it," Alex said, looking at Maria. "We actually did it."

Maria nodded a weary but triumphant smile on her face. "Yeah, we did. But we can't let our guard down. There will always be another threat."

As they walked out of the precinct, ready to face whatever challenges lay ahead, they felt a renewed sense of purpose. They had proven that justice could prevail, even against the most insidious of enemies.

And as the city began to heal from the wounds inflicted by Evelyn Chambers' reign, Alex and Maria remained steadfast, ready to protect and serve, no matter what the future held.

CHAPTER 14

UNFINISHED BUSINESS

The arrest of Evelyn Chambers, known as The Broker, sent shockwaves through the criminal underworld. With their leader behind bars, many of her associates went into hiding, while others attempted to regroup and salvage what they could of the shattered network. For Detective Alex Carter and Detective Maria Sanchez, the victory was significant, but they knew there was still much to be done.

Back at the precinct, Alex and Maria were debriefed by Captain Mitchell. The mood was one of cautious optimism.

"You both did an incredible job," Mitchell began. "But we need to ensure that every part of her network is dismantled. We can't afford to leave any loose ends."

Alex nodded. "We're already working on tracing her financial transactions and identifying any remaining key players."

Maria added, "We also need to make sure the evidence against her is airtight. She's going to have top-tier legal representation, and they'll fight tooth and nail to get her off."

As the team continued their investigation, they uncovered more details about Evelyn's operations. One troubling discovery was a list of encrypted files hinting at hidden caches of weapons and safehouses still under the network's control.

"We need to find these locations and secure them," Alex said, showing the files to Maria. "If any of her loyalists get their hands on these, they could cause a lot of damage."

Maria agreed. "I'll start decrypting these files. We need to move quickly before they realize we're onto them."

The first cache was located in an abandoned warehouse in Brooklyn. The task force executed a swift raid, seizing a large arsenal of weapons and arresting several operatives guarding the site. Each raid brought them closer to completely dismantling the network.

However, they soon realized that not all of Evelyn's associates were ready to give up. Intelligence reports indicated that a faction of the network was planning a retaliatory strike, targeting law enforcement and anyone who had cooperated with the investigation.

"This isn't over," Maria said, reviewing the intel. "They're getting desperate, and that makes them even more dangerous."

Alex clenched his fists. "We need to stay one step ahead. Let's beef up security for everyone involved and track down these remaining operatives."

As they worked to protect their own, Alex and Maria also focused on ensuring Evelyn's conviction. They compiled mountains of evidence, from financial records to witness testimonies, building an unassailable case against her.

"We have enough to put her away for life," Maria said, reviewing the case files. "But we need to make sure it sticks."

Alex agreed. "I'll talk to the DA. We need to anticipate every move her defense team will make."

Meanwhile, Evelyn Chambers was not idle. Even from her cell, she attempted to manipulate events, using her remaining influence to sow discord and confusion. Her lawyers filed motion after motion, challenging every piece of evidence and every procedural step taken by the police.

"It's like playing whack-a-mole," Alex muttered after yet another meeting with the DA. "Every time we close one door, they find another crack to slip through."

Maria was unfazed. "We just have to keep at it. She's grasping at straws, and she knows it."

The trial date approached, and the pressure mounted. The media frenzy around the case was intense, with public opinion split between those who saw Evelyn as a ruthless criminal and those who believed she was being framed.

"Stay focused," Captain Mitchell advised. "Don't let the media circus distract you. Our job is to present the facts and ensure justice is served."

As the trial began, Alex and Maria spent long hours in court, testifying and presenting evidence. They watched as Evelyn's defense team tried to undermine their case, twisting facts and casting doubt on their investigation.

But they were prepared. Each time the defense tried to poke holes in their evidence, Alex and Maria had counterarguments ready, supported by rock-solid facts and irrefutable evidence.

One evening, after a particularly grueling day in court, Alex and Maria sat in the precinct, going over their notes for the next day.

"We're almost there," Alex said, a note of weariness in his voice. "But I won't rest easy until she's convicted."

Maria nodded. "Same here. We've come too far to let it slip now."

As the trial drew to a close, the tension was palpable. The defense delivered their closing arguments, painting Evelyn as a victim of a vindictive police force. The prosecution countered with a compelling narrative of greed, manipulation, and violence orchestrated by Evelyn Chambers.

The jury deliberated for days, and the wait was agonizing. Finally, the verdict was announced: guilty on all counts.

The courtroom erupted in a mix of cheers and gasps. Evelyn remained stoic, her expression unreadable as she was led away.

Back at the precinct, the mood was one of subdued celebration. They had won a significant battle, but the war against crime was ongoing.

"Good work, everyone," Captain Mitchell said, raising a glass of sparkling water. "This is a victory for justice, but remember, we still have work to do."

Alex and Maria exchanged a look of relief and determination. They had faced one of their toughest challenges and emerged victorious, but they knew their mission was far from over.

"We did it," Maria said, clinking her glass against Alex's. "But let's stay sharp. There's always another fight ahead."

Alex nodded, his resolve unwavering. "Agreed. But for now, let's take a moment to appreciate this victory."

As they reflected on the journey that had brought them here, they felt a renewed sense of purpose. They had proven that justice could prevail, even against the most formidable foes. And as long as there were people willing to fight for it, the city of New York would remain a place where justice was not just a word, but a reality.

With Evelyn Chambers behind bars and her network dismantled, the city began to heal. Alex and Maria knew that their work would never truly be done, but they were ready for whatever came next. They had faced the darkness and emerged stronger, ready to protect and serve, no matter what challenges lay ahead.

CHAPTER 15

A NEW DAWN

With Evelyn Chambers sentenced to life in prison and her criminal network in shambles, the city of New York began to breathe easier. The streets felt safer, and there was a renewed sense of hope among its citizens. But for Detectives Alex Carter and Maria Sanchez, the end of this chapter marked the beginning of a new one.

Back at the precinct, the atmosphere was lighter. Officers shared smiles and congratulations, and there was a palpable sense of accomplishment in the air. Yet, Alex and Maria knew they couldn't rest on their laurels. They had made a significant impact, but their work was far from over.

Captain Mitchell called a meeting to discuss the next steps. "We've done a great job taking down Evelyn Chambers and her network," he began. "But we need to stay vigilant.

There are always others waiting to fill the power vacuum left behind."

Alex and Maria exchanged knowing glances. They were ready for the next challenge.

A few days later, Alex received a call from an old friend in the FBI. Special Agent Jessica Hayes had worked with Alex on several cases in the past, and she had news about a new threat.

"Alex, it's Jessica. We've been tracking a series of high-profile cyber-attacks linked to an international crime syndicate. We think they might be planning something big in New York."

Alex felt a familiar thrill of anticipation. "Tell me more. What do you need from us?"

Jessica outlined the situation: the syndicate, known as The Shadow Group, had been orchestrating sophisticated cyber-attacks on financial institutions and critical infrastructure. The FBI believed they were preparing for a major operation, and New York was a likely target.

"We need your help on the ground," Jessica said. "Your team has the local expertise we need to track these guys down and prevent the attack."

Alex agreed without hesitation. "We're in. I'll get the team together."

As Alex and Maria briefed the task force on the new threat, the energy in the room shifted. The victory over Evelyn Chambers had been sweet, but they all knew the fight against crime was relentless.

"All right, everyone," Alex said, addressing the team. "We've got a new challenge. The Shadow Group is planning a major attack, and it's our job to stop them. Let's get to work."

The task force split into teams, each focusing on different aspects of the investigation. Some tracked the cyber-attacks, analyzing data to trace the hackers' locations, while others worked on identifying potential targets in the city.

Maria and Alex focused on connecting the dots. They combed through intelligence reports, looking for patterns and clues that might reveal The Shadow Group's next move.

"These guys are good," Maria said, studying a map of recent cyber-attacks. "They cover their tracks well, but there has to be a pattern."

Alex nodded. "Let's focus on the financial institutions. If they're planning something big, they'll need money. Maybe we can catch them in the act."

Their breakthrough came when they identified a series of suspicious transactions linked to a shell company in the Cayman Islands. The company had ties to known associates of The Shadow Group, and the timing of the transactions suggested something big was imminent.

"We need to move fast," Alex said. "If they're gearing up for an attack, we have to stop them before they can pull it off."

The task force worked around the clock, coordinating with the FBI and other agencies to track the money and identify key players. Their efforts led them to an abandoned warehouse in Queens, suspected of being a staging ground for the attack.

The raid on the warehouse was executed with military precision. The task force moved in under the cover of darkness, securing the perimeter and breaching the doors.

Inside, they found a makeshift command center, complete with servers, laptops, and a dozen operatives working feverishly. The task force neutralized the operatives and secured the evidence, preventing what could have been a catastrophic attack on the city's infrastructure.

With The Shadow Group's New York cell dismantled, Alex and Maria took a moment to reflect on their victory. They had once again protected their city from a major threat, but they knew the fight was never truly over.

"We did it," Maria said, standing beside Alex as they watched the operatives being led away in handcuffs. "Another win for the good guys."

Alex smiled. "Yeah, but we can't get complacent. There's always another threat out there."

Maria nodded. "I wouldn't have it any other way."

As the city returned to a sense of normalcy, Alex and Maria continued their work, driven by the knowledge that their efforts made a difference. They had faced down some of the most dangerous criminals and emerged victorious, but their greatest strength lay in their unwavering commitment to justice.

The precinct buzzed with activity as new cases came in and old ones were solved. Alex and Maria remained at the forefront, ready to tackle whatever challenges lay ahead. They had proven time and again that they were up to the task, and they would continue to fight for their city, no matter the cost.

Late one night, as Alex sat at his desk reviewing case files, Maria approached with two cups of coffee. "I figured you could use a pick-me-up," she said, handing him a cup.

"Thanks," Alex replied, taking a sip. "You know, I was just thinking. No matter how many cases we solve, it feels like there's always another one waiting."

Maria nodded, sitting down across from him. "That's the nature of the job. But we make a difference, one case at a time."

Alex smiled. "Here's to making a difference."

They clinked their coffee cups together, a silent toast to the countless battles they had fought and the many more to come. As long as there were people willing to stand up for justice, the city of New York would always have hope.

And so, as the first light of dawn broke over the city, Alex and Maria prepared for another day, ready to face whatever challenges awaited them. Together, they were a force to be reckoned with, driven by a shared commitment to protect and serve, no matter the odds.

EPILOGUE

Months after Evelyn Chambers' conviction and the dismantling of The Shadow Group's cell, Alex and Maria continued their tireless work. The city was safer, but crime never truly slept. They remained vigilant, knowing that their efforts kept the dark at bay.

One evening, as they wrapped up another long day, Maria looked out over the city from the precinct's rooftop. "Do you ever wonder what it would be like if we could finally rest?"

Alex joined her, gazing at the skyline. "Sometimes. But then I remember that this is what we signed up for. To protect and serve. And as long as we're here, the city has a fighting chance."

Maria smiled. "To the never-ending fight, then."

"To the never-ending fight," Alex echoed.

As they stood side by side, the city sprawled out before them, they felt a deep sense of purpose. They were the unseen guardians, the ones who stood between chaos and order. And they were ready for whatever came next.

And so, the story of Alex Carter and Maria Sanchez continues with two detectives dedicated to justice in a city that never sleeps. Their journey is far from over, but with every challenge they face, they prove that courage and determination can triumph over even the darkest adversaries. Together, they remain an unbreakable force, ever-vigilant in their quest to keep New York City safe.